Usborne English Readers

Level 3

The Jungle Book

Retold by Mairi Mackinnon

Illustrated by Shahar Kober

English language consultant: Peter Viney

Contents

You can listen to the story online here:
www.usborneenglishreaders.com/
junglebook

It was a warm evening in the Indian jungle. In his cave, Father Wolf woke up, stood up slowly and stretched his legs and back. He was ready to go hunting. Mother Wolf was at the back of the cave, keeping her four cubs safe between her long nose and her strong paws.

Father Wolf listened. Among the jungle noises, he could hear something new: the low growl of a hungry tiger.

"That's Shere Khan!" Father Wolf said angrily. "How dare he come here? He'll frighten away all the smaller animals, and we have a family to feed."

"It's worse than that," said Mother Wolf. "He hurt his leg, and now he is lame, so he can only hunt the slow, stupid cows from the villages. The villagers will light fires in the grass to make him come out, so that they can shoot him. The jungle will burn, and we will all lose our homes. Why can't he hunt more quietly?"

They heard men's voices. "Is Shere Khan hunting humans, now? He should be ashamed of himself," said Mother Wolf. The tiger's growl became a roar, and the roar became a howl.

Father Wolf went outside to see what was happening. "Oh, the fool, he was chasing a man! He has jumped into a cooking-fire, and burned his paw."

"Shh, something is coming," said Mother Wolf. Father Wolf waited. He was ready to attack, but when he saw what it was, he relaxed. Into the cave came a little child, just old enough to walk. The child went over to where Mother Wolf was lying, and lay down next to her warm body with her four cubs.

"He's not frightened at all," said Mother Wolf with surprise.

A dark shape appeared at the cave mouth. "Give that child to me!" growled Shere Khan.

"We don't take orders from tigers," Father Wolf answered angrily. "Especially man-hunters. The child came to us, and we will decide what to do with him." He knew that the cave was too narrow for Shere Khan to come in any further.

"Who are you to decide? The man-cub is mine, you thieves!"

Now Mother Wolf stood up, and she was even angrier than Father Wolf. "He came to me, Shere Khan, and he is mine. He will grow and run and hunt with my cubs, and when he is old enough he will hunt *you*. Now go, or I will make you more lame and sorry than you have ever been!"

Shere Khan knew that even he couldn't win a fight with two furious wolves, and he turned away. He looked around one last time before disappearing into the jungle. "You see what the rest of the wolf pack says about this man-cub! When they reject him, I will be waiting, and I will be hungry."

Mother Wolf wasn't listening. "Mowgli," she said gently to the child. "I will call you Mowgli."

When Mowgli and the cubs were a little older, Father Wolf brought them to the Council Rock, the place where all the wolves met. There was Akela, the pack leader, and a hundred other wolves, young and old. There, too, was Baloo, the old brown bear who taught the youngest cubs the Law of the Jungle. Mowgli sat to one side, playing with some small stones and laughing in the moonlight.

Shere Khan was walking angrily around the rock. "Give me the man-cub! He does not belong in your pack."

“Who will speak for him?” asked Akela. “If two of you speak, two who are not from his wolf-family, I say he can join the pack.”

“I will speak,” said Baloo. “Let him stay. There is nothing dangerous about a man-cub, and when he is grown, he may even help you.”

“I believe you are right,” Akela agreed.

“I will speak, if you let me,” said a different voice. It was Bagheera, the panther.

"I am not a wolf or a bear," he said, "but I think you will listen to me. Near here is a fat buffalo, which I killed only this evening. If you accept the man-cub, I will give you the buffalo." He spoke more loudly. "Only a lazy coward hunts men and their cubs, Shere Khan."

The wolves came, one by one, and looked at the boy.

One by one, they nodded and went away from the Council Rock, until only Akela, Baloo, Bagheera and Mowgli's family were left. Shere Khan roared furiously, but Mowgli paid no attention.

"It's a good choice," said Akela. "Father Wolf and Baloo, teach him well."

So Mowgli grew up with his wolf brothers and sisters, and Baloo taught him all he needed to know. Mowgli learned how to run and climb and swim, and how to speak to the animals and birds and snakes politely, with respect.

There was so much to learn! Baloo said he needed to know about every animal in the jungle, and how to speak to it in its own language. He made Mowgli repeat his lessons again and again, and sometimes Mowgli forgot what he had learned.

"You are too strict," Bagheera told Baloo one day.

"Strict? He is a man-cub, and he is alone in the jungle. If sometimes I hit him gently, to help him remember, he will thank me one day."

"*They* don't hit me," said Mowgli. "They give me fruit and nuts, and they tell me I am clever."

"Who are *they*?" growled Baloo.

"The little people with tails, who live in the trees. When you hit me earlier, they came to talk to me until I felt better."

Now Baloo was really angry. "The monkey people! They are stupid, lazy thieves. Mowgli, you must never speak to them again, do you understand?"

"Yes, Baloo," whispered Mowgli, and Baloo put his arm around him.

"You need to learn," he said more gently. "Come on, it's hot. We should rest." Mowgli lay down between the bear and the panther, and went to sleep.

When he woke, Mowgli felt himself being lifted and carried by hard, strong little hands, high into the trees. "Baloo! Bagheera!" he shouted, but his friends were too late. By the time they looked up, the monkeys were far above them, chattering and laughing. Two of the strongest carried Mowgli, swinging easily from tree to tree.

Mowgli felt sick. He was frightened to see the ground so far below, and he was angry too. He couldn't guess where they were going, and he didn't recognize the trees around him. "Baloo and Bagheera will come and find me," he thought, "but how will they know where to look?"

High above the trees he saw Chil, the hawk, and called to him in the bird-language Baloo had taught him. "Help me!" he begged. "Find Baloo and Bagheera. Tell them where I am." Chil didn't answer, but he turned and flew back over the forest.

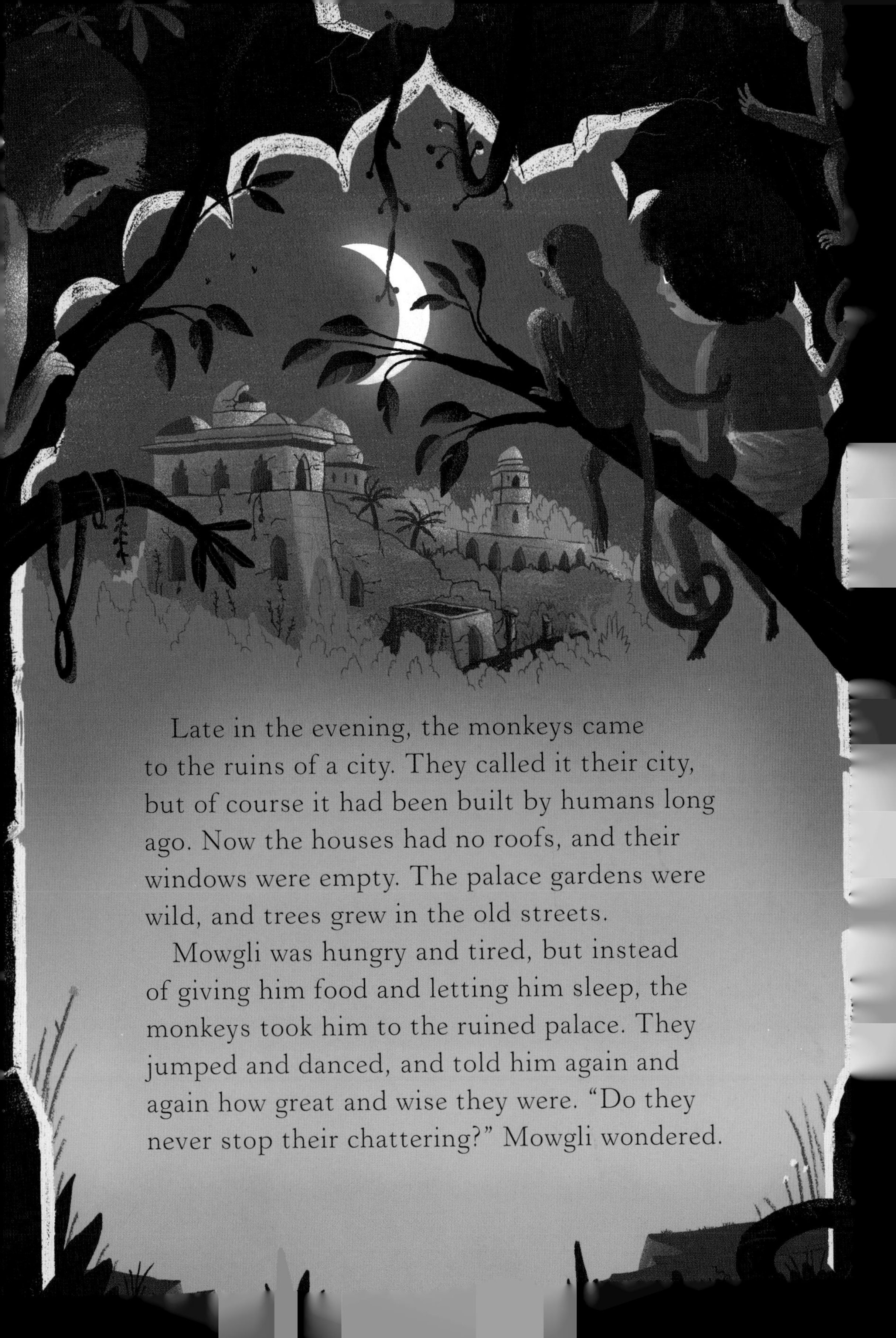

Late in the evening, the monkeys came to the ruins of a city. They called it their city, but of course it had been built by humans long ago. Now the houses had no roofs, and their windows were empty. The palace gardens were wild, and trees grew in the old streets.

Mowgli was hungry and tired, but instead of giving him food and letting him sleep, the monkeys took him to the ruined palace. They jumped and danced, and told him again and again how great and wise they were. "Do they never stop their chattering?" Mowgli wondered.

"Oh, how could I be so stupid?" moaned Baloo. He hurried after the monkeys, but a bear can't run very fast, and Bagheera was soon far ahead of him. "Stop!" said Bagheera. "We need to make a plan. The monkey people aren't afraid of us; but they are afraid of Kaa, the snake. And Kaa is always hungry."

They found Kaa, who was lying in the sun. "Good hunting to you, brother snake," said Bagheera.

"Sss. Are you hunting? Let me come too. Where are you going?"

"We are following the monkey people. They have stolen our man-cub."

"Ssss, they have no respect and no shame. Where have they taken him?"

"We don't know exactly," began Baloo; but then they heard the hawk's call from above. "I have seen Mowgli!" said Chil. "He has sent me with a message to you. He is with the monkey people in the old stone palace."

"He sent you? He has learned something, after all," said Baloo proudly. Bagheera and Kaa raced through the jungle, and even Baloo ran a little faster now.

That evening, the monkeys were still chattering to Mowgli when he saw a long black shadow behind them in the moonlight. Bagheera attacked without a sound. He hit the monkeys with his heavy paws and his terrible claws, but the monkeys rushed back at him. There were fifty monkeys against only one of him.

"Bagheera, go to the pool!" shouted Mowgli. "They won't follow you into the water."

The monkeys pulled him across the gardens to a ruined building in one corner. The jungle plants had grown so close around it that they couldn't open the doors. Instead, they climbed up to the roof and dropped Mowgli through a hole onto the stone floor. He wasn't hurt, but he couldn't climb back up, or break through the old stone windows.

Now he heard more monkey-howls, and the splash of water as Bagheera jumped into the pool, and then the roar of an angry bear. The monkeys screamed at Bagheera from beside the pool, and turned to fight Baloo.

Suddenly another long, dark shape crossed the gardens. Kaa was completely silent, and almost invisible in the darkness. He rose up to attack the crowd of monkeys around the old bear. The monkeys stopped at once, and then they all ran away in different directions, whispering one frightened word – "Snake!"

"Mowgli! Are you all right?" called Bagheera.

"I can't get out," answered Mowgli. He saw something moving outside the building, and Kaa rose up again, hitting the window with his heavy head until it broke into pieces and Mowgli could climb through.

He soon found Baloo and Bagheera. "Oh, my friends, you're hurt!" he said.

"It's nothing," they answered. "We're here, and you're alive."

Mowgli turned to Kaa. "You saved my life. Whenever I have food and you are hungry, it is yours." Then he climbed on Bagheera's back, and slept all the way home to the wolves' cave.

Ten years had passed since Mowgli had first wandered into the cave. He was with Bagheera one afternoon when the panther said to him, "Mowgli, you should be careful now. Akela is getting old, and the young wolves spend too much time with Shere Khan. Akela will protect you as long as he can, but he won't be the pack leader forever."

"But the wolves are my brothers," said Mowgli.

"Shere Khan is making them forget that," said Bagheera. "How can you show them..? I know! You need the Red Flower." He meant fire, the one thing that makes all animals afraid, but not men.

Mowgli went down the hill to the village that evening. He had often watched the villagers in their fields and houses, but he never went close. Now he saw a boy leaving one of the houses, carrying a little pot. The boy went to one of the cooking-fires, picked up some red-hot pieces of wood and put them in his pot, then covered the pot so that the fire burned more slowly.

“Is that how it’s done?” said Mowgli. He came out of the shadows like a ghost, took the boy’s pot from him and disappeared into the jungle.

Near the cave, he met Bagheera. “I have it, the Red Flower,” he said.

“That’s good,” said Bagheera. “Today Akela missed the deer that he was trying to kill. Tomorrow there will be a council meeting, and you will see that the wolves have lost their respect for Akela, so they won’t respect you either.”

All the next day, Mowgli fed his fire with branches of dry wood, and in the evening he went to the Council Rock. Akela stood on the rock for the last time.

"Brothers," he said. "You all know that I have missed my kill. That means that you can choose to fight me if you want to, and lead the pack. Who will fight?"

None of the wolves spoke. None of them dared to fight the old wolf alone. They knew that he was still powerful and dangerous.

Instead, they heard Shere Khan's voice. "Never mind the old one. Give me the man-cub that I asked for ten years ago."

"A man!" growled the wolves. "He's not one of us! Let the tiger have him!"

"What do you mean?" asked Mowgli. "I've grown up with you. I've hunted with you and I've helped you. I've pulled sharp thorns from your paws when you were hurt." But the wolves still growled, "Not one of us!"

Then Mowgli threw the fire-pot onto the ground. The fire lit some dry branches and burned bright and tall. The wolves moved back, shaking with fear. "You're not my brothers anymore!" shouted Mowgli. He picked up a branch, and ran to where Shere Khan was lying in the shadows. "And you! You once said in the Council that you would kill me when I was grown. Now I am grown, and this is what I do to my enemies!" He hit Shere Khan with the burning branch, and the tiger howled with pain.

Mowgli turned back to the wolves. "I will go away from the jungle, until I can come back to this rock with Shere Khan's tiger skin. Until then, I will not hurt you. At least *I* remember that I have grown up with you. I'm warning you, do not hurt Akela. Now get away from me!" He hit the ground again and again with his branch to make bright, hot sparks, and Shere Khan and the wolves ran away, howling.

Mowgli was left alone with his wolf family and Bagheera. Then at last he began crying, and the wolves howled with him. "Come back soon!" they called. "Don't forget us!"

Mowgli ran through the jungle until he was far away from the Council Rock. He crossed some flat land, where some buffaloes were eating the thin grass. He reached a village, where people came out to stare at him. He couldn't understand what they said, but he pointed at his mouth to show them that he was hungry.

"Such a good-looking boy!" said the village women. "Who is he?"

"Messua, doesn't he look like your son?" someone asked. "The one that was taken by a tiger?" The woman called Messua put her arms around Mowgli, took him back to her house and gave him milk and bread.

That evening she made up a bed for him, but Mowgli wouldn't sleep under a roof. Instead, he lay down in some long grass at the side of a field. Suddenly he felt a cold wet nose touching his face.

"My wolf brother!" said Mowgli. "Have you followed me all this way? Tell me, what's happening in the jungle?"

"Shere Khan is so ashamed that he has gone far away, until all his fur has grown back where you burned it. He is planning to kill you, Mowgli."

"You must tell me when he comes back. I have a plan, too."

For three months, Mowgli learned to be a man. He learned to talk, and eat cooked food, and wear clothes (which he hated). After three months, he was given a job. Now every day he had to take the buffaloes out to the fields. In the evenings, he was allowed to talk with the men in the village, although he laughed at their stories of the jungle, and especially their stories about the terrible ghost tiger. "You don't know anything! You're cowards, you're afraid of shadows. That tiger isn't a ghost! He can be killed like any other animal."

The men thought that he was very foolish, and that he should be more respectful. "If you're so clever, go and kill him yourself. The Government has offered a big reward for his skin."

"Maybe I will," said Mowgli.

Then one morning, his wolf brother woke him. "Mowgli, it's time. Shere Khan is back, and he's planning to surprise you this evening, on your way to the village."

"Where is he now?" asked Mowgli. "Oh, if only I had more of you to help me!"

"You have one more, here," said another voice.

"Akela! I knew you wouldn't forget me." Mowgli put his arms around the old wolf.

"Shere Khan is waiting for you by the river," said Mowgli's wolf brother.

"Then we can use the buffaloes to help us. Follow me!" Mowgli led the buffaloes out as usual, riding on the biggest one.

When they were a little way from the village, he called to the wolves. "We must separate the bull buffaloes from the cows and calves. Can you do that?"

The two wolves worked together like sheepdogs, running backwards and forwards among the buffaloes. The bulls snorted furiously, but Mowgli knew that the cows would be even more dangerous, because they were protecting their calves. "Brother Wolf, bring the cows down to the river and wait for me to call you."

With Akela, he drove the bulls in a wide circle around the village. The village children didn't see the old wolf, and ran home to say that the buffaloes had gone mad and run away. Then Mowgli brought the animals further down the river, to the end of a deep ravine. He knew that the sides of the ravine were too steep for Shere Khan to climb. The tiger could not escape.

"Shere Khan!" Mowgli shouted. "I have come for you!"

He drove the buffaloes forward, and Akela growled behind them, and suddenly the bulls smelled the old tiger ahead of them and charged. Shere Khan saw them, and turned to run down the ravine. Then he saw the cows waiting at the other end, and knew that he had no chance.

The furious bulls ran over him like a black wave, and charged back with the cows into the open fields… and that was the end of Shere Khan.

"Brother Wolf and Akela, Shere Khan is dead, and I need to take his skin." Mowgli began to work, until an angry voice made him look up.

"What do you think you're doing?" It was Buldeo, the village hunter. "Stop making a mess of that skin. I will take it to the Government offices, and when they give me the reward, I may share it with you."

"You *may* share it?" Mowgli laughed. "I'm not giving you the skin, Buldeo. Shere Khan is an old enemy of mine. Akela, please, this man is annoying me."

Suddenly Buldeo was lying on the ground, with an enormous wolf standing over him. "No, Buldeo, he won't hurt you unless I tell him to. Go back to the village, and stop telling me what to do."

Buldeo was terrified. He ran back to the villagers, and told them stories of tigers and a great wizard who could talk to wolves. It was evening before Mowgli had finished, and he hid the tiger skin before he reached the village.

All the villagers were waiting at the gate. "They are glad that I have killed the tiger," Mowgli thought; but then he heard angry voices.

"Wizard! Wolf boy! Go away!" Someone threw a stone.

Messua ran to him. "Mowgli, I know you're not a wizard. I know you're not my son, either, but you have killed the tiger that killed my son, and I am grateful. Now please go, or I am afraid that the villagers may kill you. Be safe!"

Mowgli shook his head. "First the wolves hated me because I'm a man, now these men hate me because I'm a wolf. This is no place for me. Brother Wolf, Akela, let me come home with you."

That night, Mowgli stretched the tiger skin over the Council Rock, and Akela lay down beside it.

"It's good that you are back," said Bagheera in his deep voice. "We have missed you."

"Be our leader again," the wolves begged Akela. "Mowgli, come back and hunt with us."

"No," said Mowgli. "You rejected me, and the humans also rejected me. Now I will hunt with my four wolf brothers and sisters, and with nobody else."

Mowgli lived in the jungle for many more years, although not for the rest of his life. Many years later, he did go back to the village, and even got married; but that is another story.

About the story

Rudyard Kipling was living in America when he wrote *The Jungle Book* in 1893-94, but his ideas came from the Indian jungle. He lived in India with his family until he was five years old, and always felt he was partly Indian. When he was a young man, he went back to India to work at a newspaper, and started writing stories.

The adventures of Mowgli and the jungle animals are some of Kipling's most famous stories. Kipling said that Mowgli means 'frog'. Mother Wolf and Father Wolf call him that because he doesn't have fur like the wolf cubs, and he always jumps about and never sits still. The stories were very popular and, in 1895, Kipling wrote a second *Jungle Book*.

Today, most people know about Mowgli from the Disney movies, made in 1967 and 2016. In the movies there are some new characters, like King Louie, the monkey king. He sings the song *I Wanna Be Like You*, and asks Mowgli to teach him the secret of fire.

Activities

The answers are on page 48.

What does Mowgli say?

Choose a word from the list to finish each sentence.

buffaloes **brothers** **wolf**
enemies **thorns**

What happened when?

Can you put the pictures and sentences in order?

A.

Mowgli took the Red Flower from the village.

B.

Mowgli's wolf brother said that Shere Khan was back.

C.

Mowgli lived in the jungle for many more years.

D.

In the village, everyone stared at Mowgli.

E.

Mowgli lay down next to Mother Wolf's cubs.

F.

Mowgli hit Shere Khan with a burning branch.

G.

"He's not one of us," the wolves growled.

H.

The furious buffaloes ran over Shere Khan.

I.

Baloo taught Mowgli the Law of the Jungle.

The jungle animals

Match the animals to the things they said.

Where are they?

Look at the pictures, then add the missing words.

Mowgli, Baloo and Bagheera were asleep ...1... the ground. Mowgli was ...2... his two friends. The monkeys were ...3... the trees, high ...4... them.

in between

on above

Kaa rose ...5... to attack the monkeys who were all ...6... Baloo. The monkeys ran ...7... in different directions.

around up

away

Mowgli's choices

Answer yes or no to the questions below.

1.

Does Mowgli choose to run away with the monkeys?

2.

Does Mowgli take the Red Flower from the village?

3.

Does Mowgli use the Red Flower to help the wolves?

4.

Does Mowgli save Shere Khan's life?

5.

Does Mowgli take the tiger skin to the government office?

6.

Does Mowgli become the wolves' leader?

Word list

ashamed (adj) if you do something bad, and then you feel bad about it, you are ashamed.

beg (v) to ask for something that you desperately want.

branch (n) a part of a tree.

buffalo (n) a type of large cow.

calf (pl **calves**) (n) a young cow or buffalo.

charge (v) when a group of animals charges, they all run forward together suddenly.

chatter (v) to talk quickly or about things that are not important.

claws (n) the sharp hooks on an animal's paws that it uses to catch smaller animals, to fight or to climb trees.

council (n) a group that makes decisions together about how to manage or organize something.

coward (n) someone who isn't brave and who avoids danger.

cub (n) a young wild animal, especially a wolf, fox, lion or bear.

deer (n) a kind of wild animal that lives in hills and woods. Other animals often hunt deer.

furious (a) very angry.

go mad (v) to become insane, or to behave in a strange way that can't be explained.

growl (n, v) when an animal growls, it makes an angry noise in its throat.

hawk (n) a type of bird that hunts small animals like mice.

howl (n, v) when dogs or wolves howl, they make a long, sad noise.

jungle (n) a tropical forest.

lame (a) when you are lame, your foot or leg is hurt so that it is difficult to walk.

lift (v) to pick something or someone up and carry them through the air.

light (v) **lit** to make a fire start.

moan (v) to make a noise that shows you are unhappy or in pain.

pack (n) a group of wolves, made of several families that hunt together.

panther (n) a large black wild cat, similar to a leopard.

pay attention (v) when you pay attention to something, you watch or listen because it is important to you.

paw (n) an animal's foot, especially a dog, cat, tiger or wolf.

ravine (n) a deep, narrow valley with steep sides.

reject (v) the opposite of accept; to show or tell someone that you don't want them.

rise up (v) when something rises up, it starts low or near to the ground, and then becomes higher or makes itself taller.

roar (n) a loud noise made by a large animal, like a lion or a tiger.

snort (v) to make a loud, angry sound through your nose.

spark (n) a tiny piece of something that burns very brightly, and that rises above a fire or falls outside it.

splash (n) when something falls into water, there is a splash.

stare (v) when you stare, you look at something hard or for a long time.

stretch (v) 1) to push your arms or legs out, especially when you have just woken up; 2) to make something fit over a larger space.

thorn (n) a sharp point on a plant.

Answers

What does Mowgli say?

1. brothers
2. thorns
3. enemies
4. buffaloes
5. wolf

What happened when?

E, I, A, G, F,
D, B, H, C

The jungle animals

Mother Wolf – F
Akela – D
Shere Khan – B
Bagheera – A
Baloo – E
Chil – C

Where are they?

1. on
2. between
3. in
4. above
5. up
6. around
7. away

Mowgli's choices

1. No
2. Yes
3. No
4. No
5. No
6. No

You can find information about other Usborne English Readers here: www.usborneenglishreaders.com

Designed by Laura Nelson
Edited by Jane Chisholm
With thanks to Rosie Hore
Digital imaging: Nick Wakeford

Page 40: Portrait of Rudyard Kipling © National Trust Photographic Library/ John Hammond via Bridgeman Images

First published in 2017 by Usborne Publishing Ltd., Usborne House, 83-85 Saffron Hill, London EC1N 8RT, England. www.usborne.com